To my immigrant parents.
And to all parents who burden and narrow their own lives in the hope that their children will be free to go further.

MY STRANGE SHRINKING PARENTS

BEING:

A PICTURE STORY
TOLD IN 38 PAGES

Written & drawn by

ZENO SWORDER

MMXXII

T&H

It goes without saying that all children believe their parents to be strange.

Mine were more unusual than most.

Before I was born, my parents had
come from far-off lands.

They had old shoes and empty pockets.

Like all good parents, they did their
best to hold me safely above the
daily troubles they faced.

My father carved me beautiful toys
from cedar branches.

My mother would quietly
sing me to sleep.

Can I tell you a secret
That every heart knows

Love is a circle
Round and round it goes

And my love for you grows
Beneath this proud skin

Though our lives may be humble
We are giants within

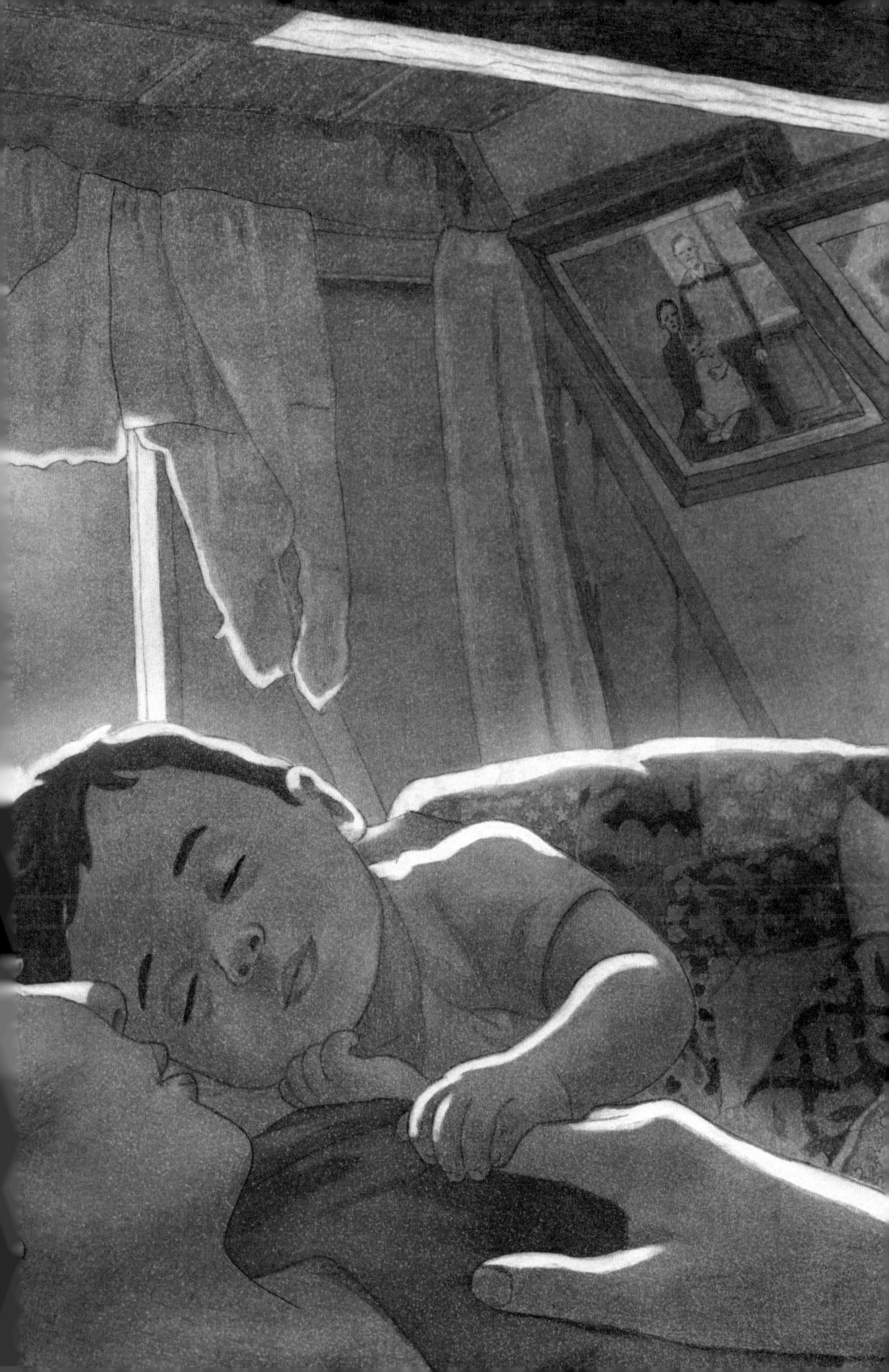

Every morning, my parents would go
to work in the city.

They struggled to get by.

Still, they tried to give me the
same as the other children.

For my third birthday, my parents went to see the baker.

R
QUALITY
PASTRIES

“We would like to buy a beautiful birthday cake but we can’t afford your price. Is there something we can trade with you?” my parents asked.

"Two inches should do it,"
said the baker.

"Two inches of what?"
they asked.

"Your height, of course,"
replied the baker.

A few years later, when I was old enough for school, the principal kindly requested only three inches for each year of schooling.

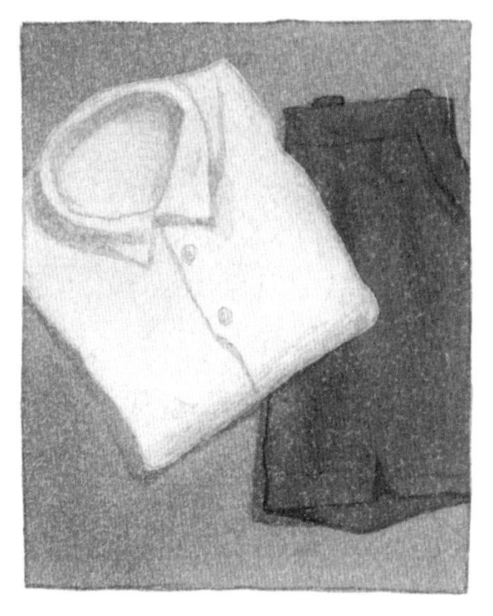

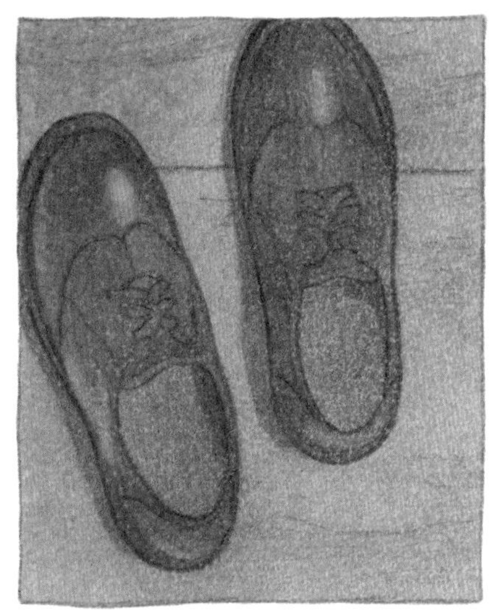

Then there was
the uniform...

shoes...

and books.

As the years passed I grew taller...

my parents shrank further and further.

Of course, there were good things about having short parents.

Running races were much more fun (sometimes I even let them win).

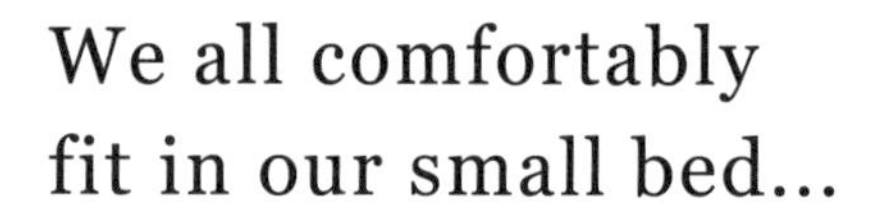

We all comfortably fit in our small bed...

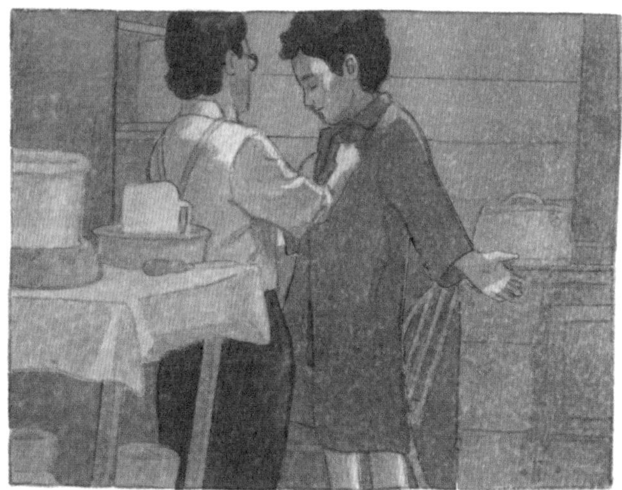

and could share the same clothes.

Most importantly, there was more room for
dancing in the kitchen.

My parents continued to shrink. Even though their work became harder they kept on going.

"This is the shape of our lives now," they told each other.

But as I grew older the children began calling me names. Their words made my chest ache. I didn't want us to be different. I was as sure as a boy could be that this was all my parents' fault.

I pleaded with them to stop shrinking, to be just like all the other parents.

I could feel my mother's chin tremble as she told me, "Those children think we're different but we're not."

"Our hearts are just as big."

"Our love is just as good."

My parents continued to give. Their world became smaller. I couldn't stop it from happening.

I began my first job as soon as I finished my studies.

I was a young man who was
beginning to grow into himself.

By the time I started a family of my own, my parents were as tall as a teacup. Now there was no need for them to give anymore.

I had learned from their example to wear my differences with my back straight and my head high. Their belief in me had grown into my courage.

I built a new house for them that didn't creak or groan.

Over time, I filled that house with furniture carved from cedar branches.

On peaceful afternoons,
when the wind settled
and the trees stood still,
they would venture outside.

And as they watched
the sun set beyond our
small garden,

I would quietly sing.

Can I tell you a secret
That every heart knows

Love is a circle
Round and round it goes

And my love for you grows
Beneath this proud skin

Though our lives may be humble
We are giants within

For 媽 (Ma)

This book was made with the contributions, care and hard work of many.

It was guided by the tremendous intelligence and insight of the publisher, Kirsten Abbott, and editors Jessica Levine, Lisa Schuurman, Fay Helfenbaum and Rebecca Lim.

It was brought into the world by Caitlin O'Reardon, Louise Lawson, Michelle Brasington, Jackie Money, Sally Gearon and the entire team at Thames & Hudson Australia.

It was inspired by Japanese woodblock prints by Hokusai and Hiroshige and books by Oscar Wilde, Shel Silverstein and Stan Sakai. Over a lifetime their pictures and words have helped me to both lose myself and find myself.

Finally, it was made possible by my wife, Renchen, my daughters, Lelea and Maya, and my big sister, Zoe. Their love and support is drawn into every page.

First published in Australia in 2022
by Thames & Hudson Australia Pty Ltd
11 Central Boulevard, Portside Business Park
Port Melbourne, Naarm, Victoria 3207
ABN: 72 004 751 964

First published in the United Kingdom in 2023
By Thames & Hudson Ltd
181a High Holborn
London WC1V 7QX

First published in the United States of America in 2023
By Thames & Hudson Inc.
500 Fifth Avenue
New York, New York 10110

25 24 23 22 5 4 3 2 1

Thames & Hudson Australia wishes to acknowledge that Aboriginal and Torres Strait Islander people are the first storytellers of this nation and the traditional custodians of the land on which we live and work. We acknowledge their continuing culture and pay respect to Elders past, present and future.

ISBN 978-1-76076-123-3
ISBN 978-1-76076-295-7 (U.S. edition)

A catalogue record for this book is available from the National Library of Australia

British Library Cataloguing-in-Publication Data
A catalogue record for this book is available from the British Library

Library of Congress Control Number 2022931904

Design: Zeno Sworder
Editing: Rebecca Lim
Printed and bound in China by C&C Offset Printing Co., Ltd

FSC® is dedicated to the promotion of responsible forest management worldwide. This book is made of material from FSC®-certified forests and other controlled sources.

A Brief Note.

I apologize for this additional note when the story has already ended and the book is ready to be closed. But for those curious few who read on, I would like to explain that while this story is imagined, its foundations are the milestones of my journey from child to parent. It is a fairytale woven together with memory.

I come from immigrant parents, one from the East, the other from the West. They were both remarkable people who showed me how to be in the world and weather its hardships. My mother, who is Chinese, sacrificed consistently and tirelessly to raise her young family in a small Australian country town. I have not known another person with such a fierce will or generosity of spirit.

When I was eleven, my family moved from the country to the city and for the first time I was surrounded by children with names that were just as strange as my own. This story owes a great debt to my close circle of childhood friends who came from all over the world; Turkey, Sri Lanka, Lebanon, Egypt, Costa Rica, Greece. Many of their parents came to a new country knowing they would be displaced in a foreign land without their families or language. They embraced a hard life for themselves in the hopes of a better life for their children. In them I saw my own parents' sacrifices and I learned something about the strange nature of love; when given it enlarges both the giver and the receiver. In this way our parents were giants.